STARS VISIBLE

Nº		MAG
9	of the 1st	
35	2nd	
92	3rd	
210	4th	
528	5th	

TUPELO
Rides the Rails

written and illustrated by
Melissa Sweet

HOUGHTON MIFFLIN COMPANY
BOSTON MASSACHUSETTS 2008

7 dog years ago,
Tupelo was born.

You are here.

"To look at the stars
always makes me dream..."
— Vincent Van Gogh

Tupelo had been dumped off by the side of the road, her sock toy, Mr. Bones, tossed out after her. She was confused—she had done nothing wrong. Now where would they go?

"Everyone belongs somewhere," she said to Mr. Bones. "We'll find a place."

She picked him up and trotted off.

There was a galaxy of sounds and places to investigate, and Tupelo
followed every lead.

But it seemed no one in all creation wanted to add a scrappy dog to their tribe.

It was getting close to dinnertime when Tupelo came upon a toad. He had no room on his log for her, and she did not want to live in a swamp anyway.

"Follow your nose," he urged her. "You're a dog—if I had a schnoz like that I'd go wherever it led me."

So Tupelo sniffed the sidewalks, the grass, and the trees. A sweet stench
floated by—the scent of sweaty boots, dirty dungarees . . . dusty dogs,
and fried wieners. It was a wonderful, intoxicating potpourri. Tupelo
followed her keen nose down the hill.

Tupelo hoped she had found a wiener-fest, but in truth she had stumbled upon an ancient bone-burying ritual. The posse of dogs spotted her just as their ceremony was about to begin.

"Are you here to make a wish?" asked Frito, a tiny brown dog with huge ears.

"No," said Tupelo. "I smelled the fried wieners. But I'd *like* to make a wish," she added, thinking perhaps she could wish for this pack to be her home.

"Are you one of the BONEHEADS?" asked Zamboni, a big white dog.

"I don't *think* so," answered Tupelo.

A dog named Daffodil explained, "We're the BONEHEADS, the Benevolent Order of Nature's Exalted Hounds Earnest And Doggedly Sublime, and we're making a wish to Sirius, the Dog Star."

Dice, a spotted dog, and big Daisy chimed in: "After we make a wish, we bury a bone as an offering. It's our way of saying thanks for granting our wishes."

"It's our dogma," said Sailor Boy. "We believe it will bring us good luck and fortune."

"And good homes!" said Abe. "Maybe even a yard, with squirrels!"

"Our own beds," added Fern.
"Someone to play ball with."
That was all Frito wanted.
"Or a snazzy outfit!" Tootsie yelped.

Fraction wanted a game of fetch, and Gizmo longed for a nice walk. Zamboni just wanted to go back home.

White-footed Po nodded toward a bright star low in the sky. "There's the Dog Star, Sirius, in the constellation Canis Major, the Big Dog. Sirius follows the constellation Orion, the mighty hunter."

The BONEHEADS began chanting:

"Sirius, Sirius, exalted star,
our swami, skipper, and our czar!
We wish you may, we wish you might
grant our wishes this starry night."

Then the BONEHEADS buried their bones in the ground, eager for their wishes to come true.

Tupelo, too, wanted to make her wish, but she had no bone. Po told her she could bury her sock toy—it looked like a bone, and it just might work. But Tupelo could not leave her beloved Mr. Bones. What if she left him and Sirius did not grant her wish? What then? No, it was too daunting.

Instead, she decided to just follow the BONEHEADS.

They led her to a hobo named Garbage Pail Tex, who was sharing fried wieners from his pail. Tex fed them all, then he hurried the dogs along so they could catch the passing train.

Up hopped Frito, Fraction, and Fern, then Tootsie, Daffodil, Daisy, and Dice. Next went Abe, Zamboni, Gizmo, Sailor Boy, and Po, followed by Tupelo with Mr. Bones.

Tupelo sat at the back of the caboose as it clickety-clacked along. The
train whistled long and low. The wind blew in her face and the smells
wafted by: the fragrant bouquet of wet leaves and rubbish cans, squirrels
and swamps. A sky full of stars glided past. The caboose was warm and
safe. This was dog heaven.

Later, Garbage Pail Tex regaled them with tales of dog heroes: of Toto's adventures with Dorothy, of Krypto, Superman's valiant dog, and of Lassie and her boy Timmy.

How brave Toto was! thought Tupelo. *And how loyal Lassie was as she rescued Timmy.*

As they rode on, Garbage Pail Tex sang a ballad to settle them down for the night.

Oh, give me a bone,
and a yard I can roam,
where the kids and the squirrels all play,
where never is heard a discouraging word
and my people rub my tummy all day.
Home home with my bone... Do doo doo...
DOo doo do doo dooo....

Tupelo wished this ride would last forever.

The next morning they arrived in Hoboken, where Garbage Pail Tex had promised to work with his hobo pals to help the dogs. The hobos gathered. They shared their information and mapped out where to go.

Rewards had been posted for Zamboni and Daffodil. They were home faster than you could shake a stick.

Dice was lucky—his people had his picture in the newspaper.

Word spread of who had lost a dog, or wanted a dog.

Two hobos brought Frito and Fraction each to a new home.
The people were ecstatic to have them.

Daisy left with a family of kids, and Sailor Boy was about to embark on a new voyage.

The stars were aligning for each of the BONEHEADS.

Tupelo slowly walked away, dragging Mr. Bones.

She was on her own again.
In all the commotion, she had lost Garbage Pail Tex.
Now there was no pack, no leader, no wieners.
What would Lassie do? Tupelo wondered.
Lassie, she decided, would be brave. Toto and Krypto, too.

Tupelo made a wish.

Then she said goodbye to Mr. Bones, burying him as best she could.

She must trust Sirius to guide her, for she was one of the BONEHEADS now. She began to roam the back roads. Then the streets. When the train whistled in the distance, Tupelo headed for it.

Tupelo rode into the night alone.

The smells of the countryside wafted by: a bouquet of rubbish cans and rac-
coons, azaleas and newly mown grass. Then the aroma of dusty boots filled
her nose . . . and the scent of dirty dungarees and a whiff of fried wieners . . .

the wonderful, heavenly stench of...

Garbage Pail Tex!

"I've been looking for you," he said, and from out of his pail Tex drew, skanky as ever, her beloved Mr. Bones. Tupelo's tail whipped around like a propeller. Then Garbage Pail Tex sat down alongside Tupelo and they watched the spinning stars.

Like Sirius and Orion, they would travel the world together, side by side . . .

. . . with a little stench.

ABOUT SIRIUS

Sirius is the brightest star in our night sky, outshining all its neighbors. It can be found in the constellation Canis Major, Big Dog, and is also known as the Dog Star. Sirius seems so bright because it's close, cosmically speaking, at only 8.5 light-years away. The best time to see Sirius (in the northern hemisphere) is from December to April. For more information about Sirius and the constellations, see *Find the Constellations* by H. A. Rey.

You are here. In the time it took you to make the journey through this book, Sirius moved 5 degrees to the west (about three finger widths of an outstretched hand) as Earth turned 345 miles eastward (at the equator). Earth orbited around the sun 22,000 miles as the spiral arm of the Milky Way galaxy carried us 180,000 miles back toward the south.

Source:
Vincent van Gogh, letter to Theo van Gogh, c. July 9, 1888, in *Letters of Vincent van Gogh, 1886–1890*, trans. and ed. by Robert Harrison (Scolar Press, 1977). Website: webexhibits.org/vangogh/letter/18/506.htm.

To my brother, **Sandy**, a legend among border collies

And to my editor, **Ann**, for whom I thank my lucky stars

And to those in my personal constellation:
Alfred, Deb, Debby, Gail, Karen, Jean, Mia, Mimi, Liz, Nan,
Sheila, my folks, Mark, Emily, and our dogs, Rufus and Nellie.
I couldn't have done it without you.

www.houghtonmifflinbooks.com ISBN-13: 978-0-618-71714-9

The text of this book is set in Kosmik. The illustrations are watercolor and mixed-media.

Library of Congress Cataloging-in-Publication Number: 2007012924   Printed in China WKT 10 9 8 7 6 5 4 3 2 1